GOODNIGHT, GRIZZLE GRUMP!

By Aaron Blecha

SCHOLASTIC INC.

ISBN 978-1-338-08829-8

12 11 10 9 8 7 6 5 4   16 17 18 19 20 21

Printed in the U.S.A.   40

First Scholastic printing, November 2016

The artist used Prismacolor Col-Erase Carmine Red and Blue
pencils on Strathmore Bristol Vellum and Photoshop
to create the illustrations for this book.
Typography by Rachel Zegar
Hand lettering by Aaron Blecha

For Betsy & Olive—
my two greatest
creations

Deep in the dark forest, where no man has
ever set foot, lives a creature quite grouchy
who goes by the name of . . .

Autumn is here and it's time
for Grizzle Grump to hibernate.

So with a polite

Grizzle Grump shuffles off in
search of a quiet place to sleep.

After finding the perfect spot in the trees . . .

Grizzle Grump
SCRATCHES
and he
SNIFFS,

then he
TEETERS
and he
TOTTERS.

Next he
WIGGLES
and he
WOBBLES,

he
FLIPS

and

FLOPS!

Finally he
SNOOZES
and
SNORES....

GRZZZZ

NIK
NOK
NIK
NOK

With a
grumble!

And a
mumble!

Grizzle Grump lumbers off in
search of a quieter place to sleep.

"This stream looks like a peaceful place for a long winter snooze!"

After finding the perfect spot next to the brook . . .

Grizzle Grump
SCRATCHES
and he
SNIFFS,

then he
TEETERS
and he
TOTTERS.

Next he
WIGGLES
and he
WOBBLES,

SCRATCH
SCRATCH
SCRATCH

he
FLIPS

and
FLOPS!

Finally he
SNOOZES
and
SNORES....

GRZZZZ

WHAP
WHUMP
WHAP
WHUMP

WHAP
WHUMP

WHAP
WHUMP

With a
moan!
And a
groan!

Grizzle Grump stumbles off in
search of a quieter place to sleep.

AHA!

"I'm sure to sleep like a log
in this dark, gloomy swamp!"

After finding the perfect spot in the marsh . . .

Grizzle Grump
SCRATCHES
and he
SNIFFS,

then he
TEETERS
and he
TOTTERS.

Next he
WIGGLES
and he
WOBBLES,

SCRATCH
SCRATCH

he
FLIPS

and
FLOPS!

Finally he
SNOOZES
and
SNORES. . . .

GRZZZZ EEERP
MEERP
EEERP
MEERP

With a
huff!

And a
puff!

Grizzle Grump stomps off in
search of a quieter place to sleep.

"Surely there's somewhere here on this high mountaintop where I can take my long winter nap!"

AHA!

"A nice, warm, quiet cave!"

Tired out and trembling,
Grizzle Grump stumbles in.

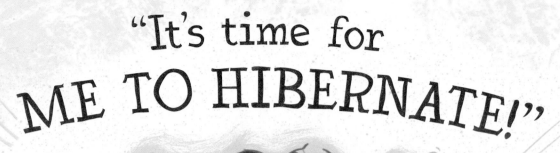

"It's time for
ME TO HIBERNATE!"

Finally Grizzle Grump falls into a deep sleep. His loud snores echo out of the cave and throughout the woods.

"Sweet dreams,
Grizzle Grump!"